Chapter 1

The hall at North Street School was buzzing with excitement. Who had won the Junior Pop Band competition? That's what all the kids wanted to know. Six bands had entered. One of them was Eric's. And he was one of the crowd, staring up at the empty stage.

'How do you think we did?' he whispered in Wesley's ear.

Wesley shrugged. 'OK, I suppose.'

'Only OK?' said Eric, whizzing
round to face him. 'Only OK?'

Wesley grinned. 'You were brilliant,
Ez. You're really cool on the guitar.'

'So you think we might win, eh
Wez?'

'Yeah. We were loads better than the
other bands. And Brent Dwyer's lot
were rubbish.'

Eric was about to say something
meaningful and modest when he felt a
hand grab hold of his neck.

Eric and the VOICE of DOOM

BARBARA MITCHELHILL

Illustrated by Bridget MacKeith

Andersen Press • London

For the girls of Seaton House School,
– especially Karis, who thought of the blanket
(B.M.)

To Morgan & Martha

First published in 2002 by
Andersen Press Limited,
20 Vauxhall Bridge Road, London SW1V 2SA

Reprinted 2004

www.andersenpress.co.uk

Text © 2002 by Barbara Mitchelhill
Illustrations © 2002 by Bridget MacKeith

The rights of Barbara Mitchelhill and Bridget
MacKeith to be identified as the author and illustrator
of this work have been asserted by them in accordance
with the Copyright, Designs and Patents Act, 1988.

British Library Cataloguing in Publication Data
available
ISBN 1 84270 108 8

Phototypeset by Intype London Ltd
Printed and bound in Great Britain by
Bookmarque Ltd, Croydon, Surrey

Class No. _____ J 5-8 _____ Acc No. C| 206230

Author: Mitchelhill: B Loc: _____

J 5-8 C|206230

1. This b~~ook~~ three weeks. It is to be
   ~~returned on the~~ last date stamped below.
   ~~A fine will be cha~~rged for every week or part
   ~~of a week overd~~ue.   (Code 23)

Other TIGERS by Barbara Mitchelhill

'Are you saying my band's rubbish?' growled Brent Dwyer who was standing behind them. Eric's blood ran cold. Brent squeezed tighter and the air in Eric's windpipe was almost cut off. He had Wez, too. So they both dangled in Brent's grasp like a pair of turnips.

'You won't win,' he said, bashing them together. 'No way!'

Eric was on the verge of passing out for lack of oxygen, when Mrs Cracker (known as the Big Cheese) marched onto the stage. Brent let go and Eric and Wez dropped to the floor as Craig Newman (lead singer with The Power) followed the Head. Some of the girls were even screaming and pretending to faint.

'Pathetic!' said Eric under his breath.

The Big Cheese flapped her hands for everyone to calm down.

'This has been an exciting afternoon,' she said, beaming down at the crowd of faces.

'Craig has listened
to the bands and now
he will tell you who
has won through to the final.'
Eric nudged Wez and
grinned as the pop star
walked to the front of the
stage.

Then there was more girlie
screaming.

'I wish they'd shut up,' said
Eric. Wez agreed.

Eventually, after a lot of
shushing, the hall went quiet.

'I'll list the bands one by one,' Craig
said. And he did. Slowly and carefully.
Describing good points and bad
points.

'This is dead boring,' Eric
whispered. 'Why doesn't he just say
who came first?'

At last, Craig pulled a gold envelope
from his pocket containing the name
of the winner. They all held their
breath as he passed it to Mrs Cracker.

'Oh my goodness!' the Head
giggled. 'This is just like the Oscars!'

She tore it open and took out a piece of paper. 'The winner is . . .' she said dramatically, 'Eric Braithwaite and his band – The Ez Effect.'

The cheers were nearly as loud as they had been for Craig Newman. But Eric noticed that nobody screamed or fainted.

'Good old Ez,' they shouted, slapping him on the back as he pushed through the crowd. Then, Wez (who played second guitar) and Kylie Partridge (drums) and Kelvin Thomas (keyboard) followed him onto the stage.

'Well done, guys!' said Craig as he shook their hands and handed Eric the silver Area Winner's Plate.

It was the best day of Eric's life – so far. This was what he wanted. A chance to be a pop star. If everything went well from now on, he'd soon be on the telly!

Chapter 2

After school, Eric had tea at Wez's house. His mum did terrific chips – brown and crisp outside and soggy inside. Just the way he liked them.

'How's your mum today?' Mrs Robertson asked as she passed the tomato ketchup. 'I expect she's feeling really tired.'

Eric looked up. 'OK, thanks,' he said and loaded his fork with a small mountain of chips.

Why was it, he wondered, that everybody asked about Mum? Nobody asked how *he* felt. If they had, he would have said:

1. It was embarrassing that Mum was having a baby at her age.

2. That the thought of having a brother was a nightmare.

But nobody cared about him and he was very depressed.

Mrs Robertson smiled. 'You must be excited, Eric. It's lovely having a baby in the family!'

Wez suddenly sat up and looked alarmed. 'We're not having any more are we, Mum?'

Before she could answer, the phone rang and she went to answer it.

'It's your dad, Eric,' she called from the hall.

'Ask him if you can stay late, Ez,' said Wesley.

When Eric came back into the kitchen, he was grinning.

'He's taking Mum to hospital. And guess what? He says I can stay the night at your house! Brilliant, eh? Can I sleep in the top bunk?'

'I'll toss you for it!' said Wez.

That night when they went to bed, they ate chocolate toffees, discussed being famous and twanged their guitars . . . until Wez's sister, Holly, came in, carrying a large stuffed lion.

'I want to come to your party,' she said.

Wesley was furious.

'It's not a party! Anyway, you're too young.'

'I'm five!'

'Go back to bed. We're talking boys' stuff.'

Holly stuck out her bottom lip. 'I'll tell Mum you're making a lot of noise.'

'Don't be stupid.'

'Give me a chocolate or I will!'

Wesley shook his head. 'No way!'

'I'll scream!' she said and turned to the door.

'All right!' Wez said and threw a sweet across the room. 'But it's my last one. Now go away.'

She had no intention of going away. She stood there, slowly unwrapping the gold paper.

Then Wesley's baby sister, Sammy, arrived.

'What oo doin', Hol?' she said.

'We're having a party – but you can't come. You're too young. And you can't have a sweet either. I got the last one.' And she popped it in her mouth.

WAAAAAHHHHH

Sammy's eyes grew wide with disappointment, her face crumpled and a loud wail erupted from her mouth.

Wez and Eric dived under their duvets as they heard Mrs Robertson thundering upstairs. She picked up the smallest child, grabbed the next size and marched them back to bed.

Ten minutes later, she returned.

'Wesley! Eric!' she said in an angry whisper. They pretended to be asleep. But Mum knew better. 'Upsetting the girls like that. How could you!' She went on and on until she ran out of steam. Then she walked out and switched off the light.

'Phew!' said Eric in the dark. 'Your sisters get you into rotten trouble, Wez.'

'Don't I know it!'

Eric sighed. 'Girls are a pain, aren't they?'

'The worst.'

'I'm glad Mum's having a boy.'

'How do you know?'

'Her friend did a test. She held a piece of string with a needle on the end over Mum's stomach and it went round and round.'

'Her stomach went round and round?'

'No. The needle. It's a sure sign it'll be a boy. 'She told me.'

'Well, that's all right then,' said Wez. 'Lucky you!'

And they fell asleep.

Chapter 3

The next day was Saturday. Mrs Robertson opened the bedroom door and called in.

'Eric! Are you awake, love?' She sounded friendly.

'Mmmmm,' Eric moaned as politely as he could. Being woken at nine o'clock on a Saturday was not fun.

She pulled back the curtains and painful rays of light struck Eric's eyelids.

'Wake up!' she said. 'You've got a busy day. Your dad's coming round at ten.'

Blinking at the light, Eric levered himself up onto his elbow. 'Can't I stay a bit longer, Mrs Robertson? Me and Wez were going to practise our guitars.'

'No, you can't!' she laughed. 'You've got more important things to do. You'll see.'

Then she left the room and went downstairs.

Wez, who had been woken by his mother's chatter, struggled to sit up. 'It's a bit inconsiderate, Ez. Why's he coming round this early?'

'Dunno. You can never tell why grown-ups do anything.'

When they went down to the kitchen, Mrs Robertson was singing loudly and setting cereal bowls on the table.

Before they were half way through breakfast, The Bodge arrived. (Eric always thought of him as The Bodge, even though he wasn't his teacher any more. Even though he was married to Mum.)

Eric looked up from his plate. What a shock! The Bodge looked awful! He had terrible bags under his eyes and his face looked chalk white. It was enough to put Eric off his food. It was obvious he should have stayed in bed.

'Hello, Eric,' he said. 'Did you have a good time last night?'

'Great!' Eric said, anxious to finish his breakfast. 'But I don't have to go home, do I?'

The Bodge glanced at Wesley's mum and smiled.

'I thought you'd want to come to the hospital to see the new addition.'

Eric looked puzzled but continued eating.

'*Your mum had the baby last night*!' he said, ruffling Eric's hair. 'Don't you want to see them?'

Eric wasn't keen but The Bodge was obviously expecting him to be excited.

'OK,' he said, when he'd wiped the last crumb of toast from his mouth. 'I'll go.' It was the least he could do.

At the hospital, Mum was in bed, her eyes closed. Some people have all the luck, thought Eric – having a good lie-in on a Saturday morning!

The Bodge raised a finger to his lips. 'Ssh! Mum's resting. Let's look at the baby.'

Next to Mum's bed, in a plastic box on wheels, Eric saw a tiny, shrivelled, red-faced thing with puffy eyes. It was quite a shock. Did newborn babies really look as bad as this? He had never seen anything like it – except when the school mouse had her litter last summer.

Mum woke up and smiled. 'What do you think of the baby, Eric?'

'Yeah,' he said. 'OK.' But he couldn't think of anything else.

Mum held her arms out to give him a hug. 'So you like her then?'

Eric suddenly froze.

'What d'you mean "her"?'

'Your little sister, of course,' said Mum.

'But you said it was going to be a *boy*!' Eric protested.

She shook her head. 'How could I know, duck?'

He was very upset. In fact, he was choked. Remembering last night at Wez's house, the thought of having a sister filled him with horror.

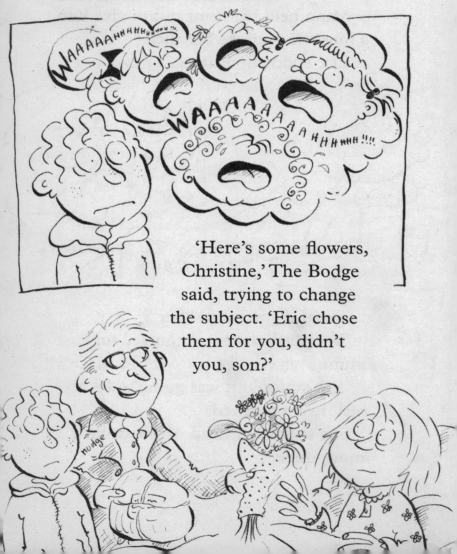

'Here's some flowers, Christine,' The Bodge said, trying to change the subject. 'Eric chose them for you, didn't you, son?'

As well as the bouquet, he handed her a parcel wrapped in brown paper.

Mum looked at the writing on the front. 'That's from Rose,' she said. 'I expect it's a present for the baby. All the way from South America.'

For the second time in ten minutes, Eric was rigid with shock. He couldn't move. He couldn't speak. A present from Auntie Rose. That's all he needed! Everything that she had sent so far had turned Eric's world upside-down. Not just that jumper he had called the Striped Horror. No, there had been more. The Wishing Stone and the Pimple Potion. And as for that fertility symbol she had sent as Mum's wedding present . . . well, here was the baby to prove its power.

Eric felt sick. This present would have serious consequences.

Chapter 4

For the next few weeks Eric had a
terrible time. Night after night, the
baby woke him with her crying. He felt
exhausted and sometimes fell asleep in
lessons. His new teacher Miss Borrage
was fantastic. She understood what he
was going through. Why couldn't Mum
be like her? She was so snappy these
days. She wouldn't even let him
practise the guitar.

'Just stop it, Eric!' she said a
hundred times a day. 'You'll wake the
baby.'

It was hopeless! The house wasn't the same. It was full of baby smells and baby noises and nappies and clothes. There was no room for his stuff any more.

The Bodge tried to help.

'How about playing your guitar in the shed, Eric? It'll be quiet there.'

But the weather was cold and he couldn't play with freezing fingers.

'I'm fed up,' he said to Wez one day. 'There's only one week to the final. We don't stand a chance if we don't practise.'

'Miss Borrage might help,' said Wez.

Eric nodded. She was his guardian angel. Of course she would help.

'I'm the leader. I'll go and ask her.'

After school, he carried her bag to the car. (He didn't care that it was extremely heavy.) Then he asked her.

'Just for you, Eric!' she said, smiling down at him. 'You can use the music room on Saturday morning.'

'Thanks!' said Eric. Miss Borrage was the best teacher ever!

When he got home, Mum was busy trying to get the baby to sleep.

'Do me a favour, Eric,' she said wearily. 'Push her round the back garden for me. Maybe she'll go off.'

Eric was in such a good mood that

32

he agreed. Mum tucked the baby in the pram and covered her with a blanket.

'I'll make myself a cup of tea,' she said. 'I haven't had one all day.'

'Can I have some crisps?' he said and Mum passed a packet over to him.

Once outside on the path, he jiggled the pram handle with one hand and dipped into the crisps with the other. The baby's eyes were closing already. Looking after babies was dead easy, he thought.

But the baby didn't fall asleep.
Suddenly, her eyes shot open and
stared at him. Maybe she was bored.
He leaned forward and jiggled a string
of yellow plastic ducks. She stared at
them and then she smiled! Eric was
very pleased with himself.

'Ducks,' he said clearly. 'Yellow
ducks.'

The baby looked up at him.

'Ducks,' Eric repeated. 'Do you like
the ducks, eh?'

The baby smiled again.

'Ooh yeth, Ewic,' she said. 'I like duckth.'

The bag of crisps fell from his grasp. His mouth dropped open. Had he heard right?

'W-what did you say?'

The baby gurgled. 'I thed I like duckth. Ethpethly yellow ones.'

It was too much for him. He abandoned the pram and ran indoors.

'MUM!' he yelled as he raced through the kitchen. 'MUM! YOU'RE NOT GOING TO BELIEVE THIS.'

Mum was sitting with her feet up on the settee and looking very tired.

'Calm down, Eric. What is it?'

'The baby's *talking*, that's what! She said she liked ducks!'

Mum sighed deeply. It was clear from the look on her face that she didn't believe a word. She swung her feet off the settee and stood up.

'Can't I even have a cup of tea in peace?' she said. 'If you didn't want to look after the baby, you should have said so.'

Eric felt miserable and retreated to his room where he sat on the bed. Had he really heard the baby speak? Or was it just that the sleepless nights were getting to him?'

Chapter 5

The Bodge was worried about Eric.
He looked tired and miserable. He
needed cheering up.

'There's a fair in town tomorrow,
Eric,' he said at tea time. 'We could all
go after school.'

Mum smiled. 'You'd like that,
wouldn't you, love?'

'Will we have to take the baby?' Eric
asked.

Mum nodded.

'Couldn't she stay at home?'

'She can't,' said The Bodge.

Eric tried arguing, but it was no use.
The baby had to come.

The next day, when tea was finished,
they got ready to go.

'Put your coat on, son,' said The
Bodge. 'There's a cold wind blowing.'

Eric fetched his padded jacket,
Mum put on her new red coat and

wrapped the baby up warm in the
buggy.

'Look at her clutching the blanket
with her little fingers,' said Mum, as
they walked down the street. 'It was a
lovely present – don't you think so,
Eric?'

'What?'

'The blanket,' she said. 'Auntie Rose
sent it.'

At the mention of Auntie Rose,
Eric's brain began to spin. He might
have guessed! The blanket had some
kind of spookiness in it. It was *that*
that made a four-week-old
baby talk.

As they walked into the fairground, Mum didn't notice Eric was distracted.

'What ride are you going on first, love?' Mum asked him.

'Dunno,' he said. 'I'll wait a bit.'

'Well, I'd like to go on the dodgems,' she laughed. 'Are you coming on with me, Brian? Eric can have the buggy for a few minutes.'

'But I . . .'

'Get yourself an ice cream, son,' The Bodge said. 'That'll cheer you up.' And he handed him some money.

Before Eric knew it, Mum and The
Bodge were whirling round in a small
red car, laughing as they bumped into
the others. Miserably, Eric pushed the
buggy a little way to the ice cream van
and bought a choc ice. It made him
feel better for a moment.

But not for long. The
baby spoke again.

'I want a duck, Ewic,'
she said.

Eric almost dropped his ice cream. He looked down at her in amazement. She was pointing towards the shooting range where yellow plastic ducks were floating on water.

'You can't have one,' he said. 'I'm not allowed to go on there.'

'Pleeeth, Ewic. I like duckth.'

'No! I said no and I mean no!'

She stuck out her bottom lip and he knew she was going to howl very loudly.

'Have some ice cream,' he said and pushed the choc ice into her hand.

She smiled and began to lick it.

'Like it!' she said.

Eric felt relieved. But in no time at all, the baby's face was smeared in brown chocolate and white ice cream.

Before he could clean her up, Mum's ride had finished and she was back.

'Eric! What have you been doing?' she said, pushing him aside. 'Babies shouldn't have ice cream. It makes them ill.'

She bent over to wipe her face.

Eric crossed his fingers, hoping the baby would speak. At least Mum would find out he'd been telling the truth, after all.

'I don't know, Eric!' said Mum. 'I can't trust you to look after your sister for two seconds.'

As Mum gave her a final wipe, the baby began to make terrible faces as if she was in pain. Suddenly, she opened her mouth and the contents of her stomach erupted all over Mum's new coat.

'Oh dear!' said The Bodge. 'She's been sick.'

'I CAN SEE SHE'S BEEN SICK!' Mum shrieked. 'It's all Eric's fault! We're going home! I've had enough!'

They turned to go and Eric wondered if life could be more miserable than this.

Chapter 6

That night, Eric lay in his bed,
thinking about the band. They were
meeting at school at ten o'clock to
rehearse for two hours. Miss Borrage
would be there and she should be dead
impressed.

'Here's to The Ez Effect!' he said to
himself. 'Winners of the Junior Pop
Band Competition! Yeah!' He smiled
and rolled over to get some sleep. He
wanted to be on top form.

Although he tried, sleep wouldn't
come. He counted a hundred sheep.
He read five comics. He ate two bags
of crisps. But nothing worked. He
couldn't stop worrying about the baby.
It seemed as if she was programmed to
get him into trouble. Like some evil
little robot.

Eventually he gave up on sleep and
sat up.

'The only thing to do,' he said to
himself, 'is to get that blanket.'

He slipped out of bed, slowly
opened the door and peeped out. The
house was quiet. The landing was dark.
Eric tiptoed towards the spare
bedroom and pushed the door open.

By the light of a small pink lamp, he could see the baby fast asleep in her cot, covered with Auntie Rose's blanket. Brilliant!

Eric leaned over and began to tug. Slowly the cover began to move but, just when he thought he had it, the baby's eyes opened.

'Ewic!' she said. 'Have you come to pway?'

'No I haven't,' he hissed. 'I came to . . . er . . . change your blanket.'

'Why?'

'Er . . . It's not suitable for a girl.'

'But I'll be vewy cold without it.'

'Well, you're too young to understand – but girls only have pink blankets.'

She stared at him and a tear trembled on her lashes. 'But I like this one, Ewic. It's vewy nithe.'

'Well, I'm going to have it,' he said and tugged hard.

The baby stared at him. 'I'll cwy!' she said and opened her mouth wide.

He knew Mum would be here like a shot if she heard. It was the worst thing that could happen.

'No!' said Eric. 'OK! OK! I won't take it.'

She closed her mouth and smiled up at him.

'All wight,' she said. 'I won't cwy.'

Eric breathed a sigh of relief and was about to go back to his room when the baby spoke again.

'Ewic,' she said. 'Will you take me to see the duckth?'

'What ducks?'

'The ones in the park.'

'When?'

'Tomowow.'

'Tomorrow? No way! I can't.'

Immediately, she screwed up her eyes and opened her mouth wide again.

'OK. OK. You win,' he said. 'But we'll have to go early. I've got a rehearsal at ten.'

'Goody!' she squealed 'You're such a luverly bwother, Ewic!'

And with that, she curled up in her cot, clutching the blanket.

Chapter 7

It was a great sacrifice! Getting up
early on Saturday morning.

By eight o'clock, Eric was dressed
and ready to take the baby to the park.
Out and back by ten. That was the
plan.

Down in the kitchen, the baby was
sleeping in her buggy, tucked up in
Auntie Rose's blanket. As Eric walked
in, she opened her eyes.

'Can we go to see the duckth now,
Ewic?' she said, smiling at him.

Eric felt irritated.

'When I've had my breakfast,' he
said.

'Now! Now! Now!'

Just then, Mum walked in through
the back door, carrying an empty
clothes basket.

'You wouldn't believe a baby could
make so much washing,' she said as
she passed through the hall. Eric
glanced at his sister. But she didn't
speak.

'Make me a cup of tea, will you,
love?' Mum called. 'I'm tired out.'

Eric sighed. She wasn't the only one!
He had hardly slept! Who would have
thought that this tiny, helpless baby
could force *him* – a grown boy – to do
things he didn't want to?

51

Then it struck him that he was
being ridiculous! Of course she
couldn't force him! What could she do
if he walked out? *Nothing*! That's what!

He went and filled the kettle and
switched it on. But when he turned
back, the buggy was empty. He
panicked. Where was she? How could a
four-week-old baby get out?

'I'm here, Ewic,' she said as if she
could read his mind.

She was sitting on the floor
on the far side of the
kitchen. Worse still – she
was holding Mum's
best crystal vase.

'Take me to the duckth, Ewic,' she said, 'or I'll dwop it.'

Eric was gobsmacked! If she smashed the vase – who would get the blame? HE WOULD! This was pure blackmail!

'All right! All right!' he said. 'I'll take you if you put it down.'

'*Now*!'

'Wait a bit. I'm making a cup of tea.'

'NOW!' she yelled holding the vase over her head.

'OK. OK!' said Eric. 'We'll go now. But I'll have to tell Mum.'

Mum walked in just as the kettle boiled. 'What will you have to tell Mum?' she asked.

Eric busied himself making the tea, hoping Mum wouldn't see his sister on the floor.

'Er . . . I was thinking of taking the baby a walk,' he said as he put the mug on the table. 'Give you a bit of a rest.'

'That is thoughtful of you, love,' said Mum and she flopped onto a chair.

Once her back was turned, Eric grabbed the baby and dumped her into the buggy.

'Right!' he said. 'I'll take her now.'

Mum looked up from her tea. 'Not yet, Eric. I've got to feed her. It won't take long. Just let me finish my cuppa.'

Eric paced the floor while Mum drank her tea . . . gave the baby some milk . . . and changed her nappy. He could have done it twenty times faster! When she had finished, it was quarter past nine. Doom! He'd have to run all the way to the park.

When he was out on the street, he suddenly felt it wasn't cool to be seen

pushing a baby. This was not how a
future pop star should behave. He
pulled his baseball cap over his
forehead. Heavy disguise! Maybe no
on would recognise him.

No such luck!

'Hey, Eric!' called a familiar voice.
'Whatcha doing with that buggy? Are
you playing Mummies and Daddies?
You look a right twit!'

It was Brent Dwyer! Of all the
people in the world, it had to be him.
Now everyone would know that ace
guitarist Ez Braithwaite was a baby-
minder. Soon he'd be a laughing stock.

Chapter 8

Eric raced towards the park, trying to make up for lost time.

'WHEEEEEEE!' cried the baby as the buggy whizzed along. 'Keep going, Ewic! I like it!'

By the time they got there, Eric was out of breath.

'This is it . . .' (gasp!) 'You can look . . . ' (gasp) 'at the ducks for . . .' (gasp!) 'five minutes . . .' (gasp!) 'and then we go home!' (double gasp!)

He left the buggy on the path where she could see the pond. Then he flopped on a bench to recover his breath and closed his eyes for a second. When he opened them again he was horrified! The buggy was heading towards the pond. The baby was sitting up, clinging onto the sides.

Eric leapt to his feet. 'Stop!' he yelled and raced after her. He had to get her before she reached the water.

But the baby was having a great time. 'Hey duckie-duckieth!' she called as the buggy zipped along the path. 'I's coming to pway wiv you.'

Then SPLASH! The buggy hit the
water. The ducks quacked in a
deafening chorus, flapped their wings
and paddled off. The buggy floated
after them.

Luckily the park keeper was on the
other side and saw what had
happened. He dived into the pond –
fully clothed.

'All right, my little lovely,' he called
as he swam through the weed-infested
water. 'I'll get you back to your
mummy soon.'

Eric raced round the pond and was
waiting when the park keeper emerged
from the pond, dripping with slimy
mud and dragging the buggy after
him. And when he saw Eric standing
there, he did not look pleased.

'Are you in charge of this baby?' he
snapped.

Eric nodded nervously.

'THEN YOU OUGHT TO BE
ASHAMED OF YOURSELF!'
he shouted. 'Where do you live?'

When Eric said, '34 Corporation Street,' the angry park keeper marched him back home.

Then . . .

The park keeper knocked on the door.

Mum opened the door.

Mum listened to the park keeper.

Mum went mad at Eric.

The park keeper went mad at Eric.

Eric was sent to his room.

GLOOM

He would never make it to the
rehearsal now!

He wasn't allowed out until twelve
o'clock. Then he raced down to school
to explain what had happened.

Wez and the rest of the band were
sitting by the gate. Brent Dwyer was
with them and some other kids he
wished would disappear.

'Well, look who it is!'
Brent Dwyer shouted.
'Only two hours late!'

'I had to . . .'

'Don't tell us any lies, Eric
Braithwaite,' said Kelvin, standing up
to face him. 'Brent saw you in the
park.'

'But . . .'

'We heard! You were playing by the
pond!' Kylie interrupted. 'Miss
Borrage is really mad with you, too!
You didn't care about the band.'

'I helped out at the rehearsal,'
sneered Brent Dwyer. 'Lucky I
brought my guitar.'

Normally, they wouldn't let Brent near the band – but they were so angry with Eric that they let him play.

Eric tried to speak.

'We don't want to talk to you,' said Kelvin. 'We just don't want you in the band.'

With that he and Kylie walked away and the rest followed.

Only Wez stayed behind.

'We're all a bit fed up, Ez,' he said. 'What really happened?'

Eric hung his head. 'It's a long story, Wez,' he said. 'It's another of Auntie Rose's presents.'

Wez nodded knowingly. 'Then it's trouble with a capital T, Ez. Tell me about it.'

They sat down on the wall and Eric explained how his four-week-old sister could talk.

'That's weird, Ez!'

'I know,' Eric continued. 'The problem is – she's blackmailing me,

now. She gets me into trouble if I
don't do what she wants. So what can
I do, Wez?'

Wesley thought for a minute.

'Easy!' he said. 'You just wash the
blanket.'

'Why?'

'Remember the Striped Horror lost
its power when it was washed?
Well . . .'

Eric's shoulders drooped. 'No good,
Wez. I can't get it. I've already tried.'

'That's bad, Ez,' said Wesley, shaking
his head from side to side. 'You're
already in trouble with the band and
Miss Borrage. It looks as if things can
only get worse.'

Chapter 9

It was the end for Eric. The band had finished with him. He was in deep trouble with everybody. And – the worst thing – he faced years of being blackmailed by his baby sister. There was only one thing to do . . .

He would leave home!

The sooner he left, the sooner Mum would find out the truth about the baby. Then she would feel really bad and spend weeks searching for him. Then, when she had found him she would fling herself at his feet – sobbing – and beg him to come home.

Suddenly, Eric felt better.

That night, he packed his sports bag, ready to go. He filled it with two bumper bags of crisps from his emergency store, his top ten favourite comics and his best football strip. At the last minute he squeezed in a spare pair of socks.

As he opened the bedroom door, he picked up his guitar. 'This should be good for busking,' he said to himself. 'I could earn a fortune!'

He stepped out onto the landing and tiptoed towards the top of the stairs. Everywhere was silent. Everyone was fast asleep . . . except the baby!

'Ewic!' she called. 'Ewic, come and pway wiv me.'

He rushed into
her room and clapped
his hand over her mouth.

'All right! All right!' he whispered.
'But don't make a sound.'

He pulled his hand away from her
startled face. Then she smiled.

'Pway me a tune, Ewic!' she said,
pointing to his guitar. 'Thing to me,
pleeeeth!'

'I can't,' he hissed. 'Mum and The
Bodge will wake up.'

The baby opened her mouth wide as
if she was about to yell.

'No!' Eric pleaded. 'Don't cry.'

'I will if you don't pway your guitar,

In desperation, he gave in.

'If you promise to be good, I'll take
you downstairs and play to you.'

The baby smiled and held up her
arms to be picked up.

Eric carried her
downstairs wrapped
in the blanket and put
her on the settee. Then
he went back and
fetched his bag and guitar.

'What's in that bag?' the baby asked
when he returned.

'Nothing.'

'Want to thee!'

Eric opened it and she saw the
crisps.

'I like cwisps,' she said.

'You're too young,' Eric protested.

'Want some,' she said and Eric gave
in, again. It was the only way to stop
her from yelling.

'Thing to me, Ewic,' she said as she took the first crisp out of the packet.

Eric decided that, if he played something quiet, nobody upstairs would hear. So he sang 'She'll be Coming Round the Mountain'.

'Again!' she said when he had finished.

He had sung it *eleven* times and was very bored indeed, when he suddenly realised she had fallen asleep. Not only that, but she had a crisp in one hand and the packet in the other. For the first time in weeks, she was not holding onto the blanket! Now was his chance.

Carefully, he tugged at it and, bit by bit, it slipped away. Once it was off, he quickly spread his football shirt over her so she wouldn't feel cold. Then he slipped into the kitchen and turned on the taps.

In less than ten minutes, the blanket was washed and Eric spread it over a chairback to dry.

'Please let it work!' he muttered

before he went back to the living room and sat next to the sleeping baby.

It was six o'clock before he woke up. Mum was standing over him holding the baby.

'What happened, Eric? I went to the baby's room and she wasn't there. I had the fright of my life!'

Eric rubbed his eyes and tried to think of something.

'Er . . . I heard her crying in the night so I brought her down and gave her a bottle. I did it just like you do.'

'Well, you do surprise me!'

'I thought you needed a good night's sleep.'

'Oh, Eric,' she said, blinking away a tear. 'You can be so helpful.'

Then he remembered the blanket.

'Oh yes . . . She was a bit sick. You know how babies are. So I washed that cover thing Auntie Rose sent her.'

Mum was so impressed that Eric changed his mind about running away. Maybe things had started to look up.

Chapter 10

As it turned out, the baby didn't speak
to Eric again. The washing must have
worked.

'That's a load off your mind, Ez,'
said Wesley when they met in the park
on Sunday.

'But what about the band, Wez? Am
I really out of it?'

'No way!' Wez said as he slapped
Eric on the shoulder. 'I talked to Kylie
and Kelvin yesterday. Told them you
were having a bad time 'cos of the new
baby. Kelvin said his mum was really
ratty when their baby was born. Kylie
said the same. They know what kids
have to put up with, Ez.'

It was a great relief!

After that, things began to go smoothly. The baby slept during the night and Eric's band rehearsed at Kelvin's house. All was well.

The final of the Band Competition was to be held on Saturday.

At eight o'clock, Wez's mum arrived to pick him up in her car.

'We'll see you later, Eric,' said The Bodge as they waved him off.

'Good luck!' Mum called.

At the theatre, they were shown around and were allowed to go onto the stage to see how it felt. It was large and square and lit by huge bright lights. They walked around trying to take it all in.

'Wow!' said Eric. 'This is cool!'

Kylie grinned and nodded. 'Now I know what it feels like to be famous!'

But Wez and Kelvin were more nervous than they had ever been in their lives.

When the competition started, The Ez Effect was to be the last band to play. When it was almost time to go on stage, they stood in the wings waiting for their turn, peeping through the curtain and looking at the audience.

'I can see your mum and The Bodge,' said Kelvin.

'Where?'

'Right at the back.'

Eric peered out. Sure enough, they were there and Mum was holding the baby, wrapped in Auntie Rose's blanket. No problem! thought Eric. Everything was OK now.

At that point, the stage manager called, 'Right, boys. When the last band leaves the stage, I want you to walk on.'

The Evil Five finished their number, the audience cheered and the curtains closed. Then The Ez Effect walked on.

'Good luck, guys!' said Kylie as she sat behind the drum kit. And the curtains opened.

It was the best night of Eric's life so far. He played brilliantly. As did the rest of the band. Afterwards, they went and sat in the front row waiting for the results.

The judge took his
time and made a boring
speech while Eric
squirmed with impatience.
At last, he announced, 'The
winning band is . . . The Ez
Effect.'

Eric leapt into the air ahead
like a cork from a bottle. He
jumped and cheered and
generally went wild.

Later, when they went backstage for
the celebrations, Mum, The Bodge and
the baby went, too, and made a great
fuss of him.

There was lots of food and cola and
Eric thought it was a great do.

'I think there's a reporter wants to
talk to you, Eric,' said Mum while he
was stuffing a sandwich into his
mouth. 'Just remember, you're a pop
star, now!' And she laughed.

Eric brushed the crumbs off his tee-
shirt ready to speak to the journalist.

'This is your family, is it, Eric?' the
man asked as he opened his notebook.

Eric shrugged his shoulders and
said, 'Yeah,' in a cool, pop-starish kind
of way.

The reporter jotted some notes and
then he noticed the baby. 'And who is
this little person?' he asked.

'My sister,' said Eric. 'Actually, she's
the band's mascot.' He had just
thought of that off the top of his head.
Reporters liked that kind of thing.

'Great!' said the journalist and
scribbled more notes. 'What's her
name?'

Mum leaned forward. 'We only decided today,' she said. 'We think we're going to call her Rose after my sister.'

Eric suddenly felt nervous. One Rose in the family was more than enough.

'Maybe we should talk about it, Mum,' he said.

But the baby shook her head, looked Eric straight in the eye and *winked*!